Published in the United States 1991 by
Dial Books for Young Readers
A Division of Penguin Books USA Inc.
375 Hudson Street
New York, New York 10014
Created and produced by David Bennett Books Ltd., St Albans, England
Pictures copyright © 1991 by Carol Lawson
Printed in Singapore
First Edition
1 3 5 7 9 10 8 6 4 2

Library of Congress Cataloging in Publication Data
Lawson, Carol. Teddy Bear, Teddy Bear: pictures / by Carol Lawson.
p.   cm.
Summary: An illustrated version of the familiar nursery rhyme.
ISBN 0-8037-0970-6
1. Nursery rhymes. 2. Children's poetry. [1. Teddy bears—Poetry.
2. Nursery rhymes.] I. Title.
PZ8.3L379Te 1991 398.8—dc20 90-44083 CIP AC

Teddy Bear, Teddy Bear

Pictures by
Carol Lawson

Dial Books for Young Readers New York

Teddy bear, teddy bear,
wake up now.

Teddy bear, teddy bear,
take a bow.

Teddy bear, teddy bear,
dance on your toes.

Teddy bear, teddy bear,
touch your nose.

Teddy bear, teddy bear,
turn right around.

Teddy bear, teddy bear,
touch the ground.

Teddy bear, teddy bear,
show your shoe.
Teddy bear, teddy bear,
that will do.

Teddy bear, teddy bear,
run upstairs.

Teddy bear, teddy bear,
say your prayers.

Teddy bear, teddy bear,
stand on your head.

Teddy bear, teddy bear,
go to bed.

Teddy bear, teddy bear,
turn off the light.
Teddy bear, teddy bear,
say good night.